Dedicated to the Somerville First-Time Mamas (SITM)—a group of women who support, inspire, and grow together. We are so lucky to know all of you.

-Sailaja and Amy

For Lily, Brooks, and Luke... for so much happiness.

-Tim

www.bharatbabies.com

Harini & Padmini Say Namaste

For more information, please contact:
Mascot Books
560 Herndon Parkway #120
Herndon, VA 20170
info@mascotbooks.com
namaste@bharatbabies.com

Library of Congress Control Number: 2017908688

CPSIA Code: PRT0717A
ISBN-13: 978-1-63177-848-3

Printed in the United States

bharat babies™ Presents

L2

HARINI & PADMINI SAY NAMASTE

WORDS BY AMY MARANVILLE · PICTURES BY TIM PALIN

"Are you ready for yoga?" Padmini's Amma asked.

"What's yoga?" Padmini asked.

"Yoga is an ancient Hindu form of worship," said Mama. "It is a path to the divine that requires focus from our minds, our bodies, and our spirits."

"Namaste, Padmini, and Padmini's moms," said Miss Janani.

"What does *namaste* mean?" asked Padmini.

"The divine in me bows down and recognize the divine in you," said Miss Janani.

"You see, Padmini, yoga is based on devotion, love, and concentration. When we practice yoga, we are working to become more spiritual and centered people. We are working to connect with the divine—whatever form it may take."

Padmini saw her friend Harini. She waved, and ran over to put her mat down next to her friend's.

"I didn't know you did yoga," Harini said.

"This is my first time," Padmini said. "I'm really excited!"

Miss Janani rang a small bell. "Welcome, my friends," she said as everyone sat down on their mats.

"Yoga is not just a type of exercise, but a way to enhance our spirituality. Today, we are going to practice some asanas, or physical yoga poses. We use asanas to help us tune our bodies. Let's start in *Padmasana*, or lotus position."

"I know this one!" Padmini whispered proudly.

"While we are in lotus position, try *Pranayama*," Miss Janani said. "Close your eyes and take some deep breaths. Breathe in through your nose, and then out through your mouth. Feel how closely connected you are to the world around you."

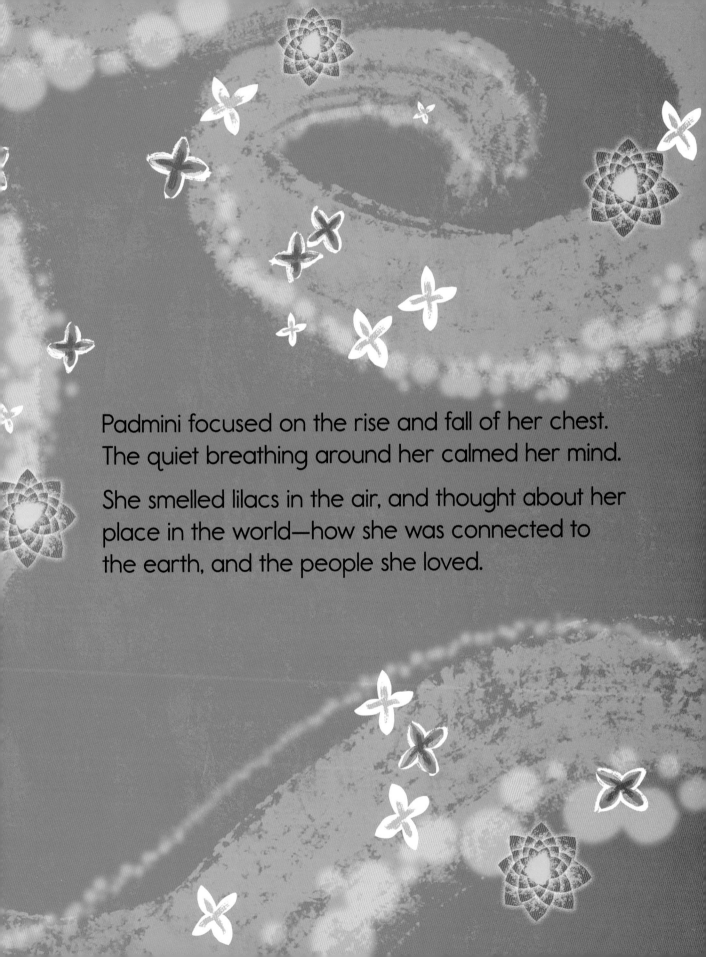

Padmini focused on the rise and fall of her chest. The quiet breathing around her calmed her mind.

She smelled lilacs in the air, and thought about her place in the world—how she was connected to the earth, and the people she loved.

"Now lean forward onto your hands and knees and come into cat pose," said Miss Janani.

Padmini's mouth dropped open. Cat pose? "Psst, Harini, what's a cat pose?"

"Pretend like you have four legs," Harini whispered, "then make your back round, like a cat when it hisses."

"Very nice," said Miss Janani. "Next, try cow pose."

"Psst, Harini! Is this how you do the cow?"

"Noooo!" Harini whispered. "Lift your head, and let out your moo!"

"I get it!" Padmini said.

"Now," said Miss Janani, "let's try downward facing dog."

Padmini giggled. "Harini, is it time to stand on our heads?"

"Nooo," said Harini. "It looks like this."

"Like this?" Padmini asked,

"Oh, like this?" Padmini asked.

"Now move your right leg forward, and come into horse-riding pose," said Miss Janani.

By the time they got to the *Malasana Squat*, Padmini was following along more easily. Her body stretched and pushed to reach the poses. She felt sweat forming on her brow, and a quiet focus as her body and mind worked together.

Finally, the class came into Savasana, resting pose. As she lay on her back, breathing deeply, Padmini felt her spirit shine in the peaceful quiet of the moment. Her body was tired, but her mind and spirit were wide awake.

"That was tough," Padmini said, as she rolled up her mat, "but I can't wait to do it again—I have a lot of poses to practice!"

Miss Janani smiled. "You'll only get better as you practice. Remember that yoga is a lifelong skill. With time and patience comes greater wisdom. *Namaste*, Harini and Padmini!"

"*Namaste*, Miss Janani," the girls said.

Yoga is thousands of years old and came from India. It's also one of the six schools of Hindu thought.* Yoga means "to unite" and is a path to grow closer to God. *The Bhagavad Gita*, a famous Hindu scripture, discusses four types of yoga: *karma* yoga, dedicating all actions and thought to God; *jnana* yoga, intense study of scripture; *bhakti* yoga, the worship of God by loving all beings; *dhyana* (*raja*) yoga, the path of meditation. All four paths are interconnected, but a person's unique personality draws them more closely to one than others.

Dhyana (Raja) yoga has the most in common with how yoga is understood today. It involves the practice of *asana*, or physical posture, and *pranayama*, or breathing. While the practice of *asana* and *pranayama* has health benefits, such as lowering blood pressure and boosting the immune system, they are tools in the larger system of yoga to help one grow closer to God. Anyone can practice yoga.

—Sheetal Shah
Senior Director, Hindu American Foundation

The six major schools of Hindu thought are Samkhya, Yoga, Nyaya, Vaisheshika, Mimamsa, and Vedanta.

Pronunciation Guide

Hi friends, you might notice that our pronunciation guide is a little different from other guides. We use familiar words to make pronunciations easier and more accessible. We hope this helps you learn more about the amazing cultures, religions, and people from South Asia.

Yoga: yo-gaa
An ancient Hindu all-encompassing form of worship

Padmini: pa-dh-mi-nee

Amma: a-mm-aa
Another term for mother in many South Asian languages

Hindu: hin-dh-oo
An individual who practices Hinduism

Namaste: nah-mah-stay
Traditional Sanskrit greeting meaning "The Divine in me bows down and recognizes the Divine in you"

Janani: ja-naa-nee

Harini: haa-ri-nee

Asana: aa-saa-naa
Physical poses done in yoga

Padmasana: pu-dh-maa-saa-naa
Lotus pose

Pranayama: praa-naa-yaa-maa
Breathing exercises done in yoga

Malasana: mal-aa-saa-naa
Squatting pose

Savasana: saa-vaa-saa-naa
Resting pose